A book
is a present you can open
again and again.

THIS BOOK BELONGS TO

FROM

THREE LITTLE PIGS

Adapted from an English folk tale

General Editor
Bernice E. Cullinan
New York University

Retold by
Seva Spanos

Illustrated by
James Eugene Sutton

TREASURE TREE ™

World Book, Inc.
a Scott Fetzer company
Chicago　　London　　Sydney　　Toronto

ISBN 0-7166-1602-5
Library of Congress Catalog Card No. 91-65470
8 9 10 11 12 13 14 15 99 98 97 96

Cover design by Rosa Cabrera
Book design by PROVIZION

ONCE UPON A TIME, there was a mother pig with
three little pigs. One day, the three little pigs decided
to leave their home to go seek their fortunes.

THE FIRST LITTLE PIG met a woman with some bundles of straw and said, "Please, will you help me get some straw to build my house?"

"What!" the woman said. "I know I never saw a house made all of straw. But if only that will do, I'll give this straw to you. I'll help you build it too, little pig."

"Yes, yes," replied the first little pig. "And I thank you!" And the two worked together to build the house of straw. Then the woman went on her way.

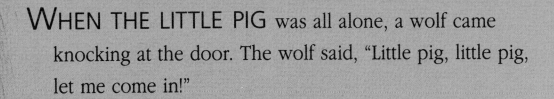

WHEN THE LITTLE PIG was all alone, a wolf came knocking at the door. The wolf said, "Little pig, little pig, let me come in!"

The little pig squealed, "No, no, no! Not by the hair on my chinny chin chin!"

"Then I'll huff and I'll puff and I'll blow your house in!" replied the wolf.

So THE WOLF huffed and puffed and blew the straw house in. And the first little pig ran away.

THE SECOND LITTLE PIG met a man with a cart of sticks and said, "Please, will you help me get some sticks to build my house?"

"What!" the man said. "A stick house isn't strong, and won't last very long. But if only that will do, I'll give these sticks to you. I'll help you build it too, little pig."

"Yes, yes," replied the second little pig. "And I thank you!" And the two worked together to build the house of sticks. Then the man went on his way.

WHEN THE LITTLE PIG was all alone, the wolf came knocking at the door. The wolf said, "Little pig, little pig, let me come in!"

The little pig squealed, "No, no, no! Not by the hair on my chinny chin chin!"

"Then I'll huff and I'll puff and I'll blow your house in!" replied the wolf.

So THE WOLF huffed and puffed and puffed and huffed. At last, he blew the stick house in. And the second little pig ran away.

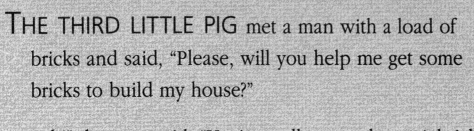

THE THIRD LITTLE PIG met a man with a load of bricks and said, "Please, will you help me get some bricks to build my house?"

"Ah!" the man said. "You're really very clever. A brick house lasts forever! Since only that will do, I'll give these bricks to you. I'll help you build it too, little pig."

"Yes, yes," replied the third little pig. "And I thank you!" And the two worked together to build the house of bricks. Then the man went on his way.

WHEN THE LITTLE PIG was all alone, the wolf
came knocking at the door. The wolf said, "Little pig,
little pig, let me come in!"

The little pig squealed, "No, no, no! Not by the
hair on my chinny chin chin!"

"Then I'll huff and I'll puff and I'll blow
your house in!" replied the wolf.

WELL, the wolf huffed and puffed and puffed and huffed and huffed and puffed again. But he could not blow the brick house in. So the wolf changed the subject and said, "Little pig, I know where we can find a field full of fat, tasty carrots."

"Where?" asked the little pig.

"At the farm next door. Be ready tomorrow morning, and we will go pull some carrots for lunch. After all, it's no fun to eat alone." Then the wolf smacked his lips.

"Oooh!" the little pig thought. "I know just what he'll do —make little piggy stew. So early in the day, I'll play this game my way." And the little pig said, "OK, I'll go too."

"Yes, yes," replied the wolf. "And I thank you! We'll leave at six o'clock sharp."

WELL, the little pig left at five o'clock instead, pulled the carrots, and was back home before six. Soon the wolf came knocking at the door and said, "Little pig, are you ready?"

"Ready?" replied the little pig. "I've gone and come back again. I already have a potful of fat, tasty carrots simmering in my fireplace."

The wolf was annoyed, but he knew there must be *some* way to trick the little pig. So the wolf said, "Little pig, I know where we can find a tree full of big, crispy apples."

"Where?" asked the little pig.

"In an orchard on the far side of town. Be ready tomorrow morning, and we will go pick some apples. I want to make apple jelly for our breakfast toast. After all, it's no fun to eat alone." Then the wolf smacked his lips.

"Oooh," the little pig thought. "I know what he wants most—piggy sausage with his toast. Once more I'll use my trick—get there and back real quick!" And the little pig said, "OK, I'll go too."

"Yes, yes," replied the wolf. "And I thank you! We'll leave at five o'clock sharp."

WELL, the little pig left at four o'clock instead, hoping to get back home before the wolf came. But the orchard was far away, and the little pig had to climb a tree to pick the apples. Just as the little pig was climbing back down, the wolf appeared. This time, he was angry, but he knew there must be *some* way to trick the little pig. So the wolf said, "Little pig, I see you got here ahead of me. How are the apples?"

"Very big and crispy," replied the little pig. "Here's one for you." And the little pig tossed the apple away from the tree. When the wolf ran to get it, the little pig jumped down and raced home.

THE NEXT DAY, the wolf appeared again. This time, he was furious. But the stubborn wolf would not give up. He just *knew* there must be some way to trick the little pig. So the wolf smiled and said, "Little pig, I know where there is a wonderful fair going on today."

"Where?" asked the little pig.

"Nearby in town. Be ready this afternoon, and we will go try a slice of the very best pie at the fair. After all, it's no fun to eat alone." Then the wolf smacked his lips.

"Oooh," the little pig thought. "I know just what he'll try—a little piggy pie. But he would never dare to eat me at the fair." And the crafty little pig said, "OK, I'll go too."

"Yes, yes," replied the wolf. "And I thank you! We'll leave at three o'clock sharp."

WELL, the little pig left at two o'clock instead, got to the fair, and bought a great big barrel. On the way home, the wolf appeared up the road, just as the little pig had thought he would. The little pig hid in the barrel, and soon it began to roll. The barrel rolled down the hill with the little pig squealing and oinking and oinking and squealing and screaming and scaring the wolf so badly that he ran straight home.

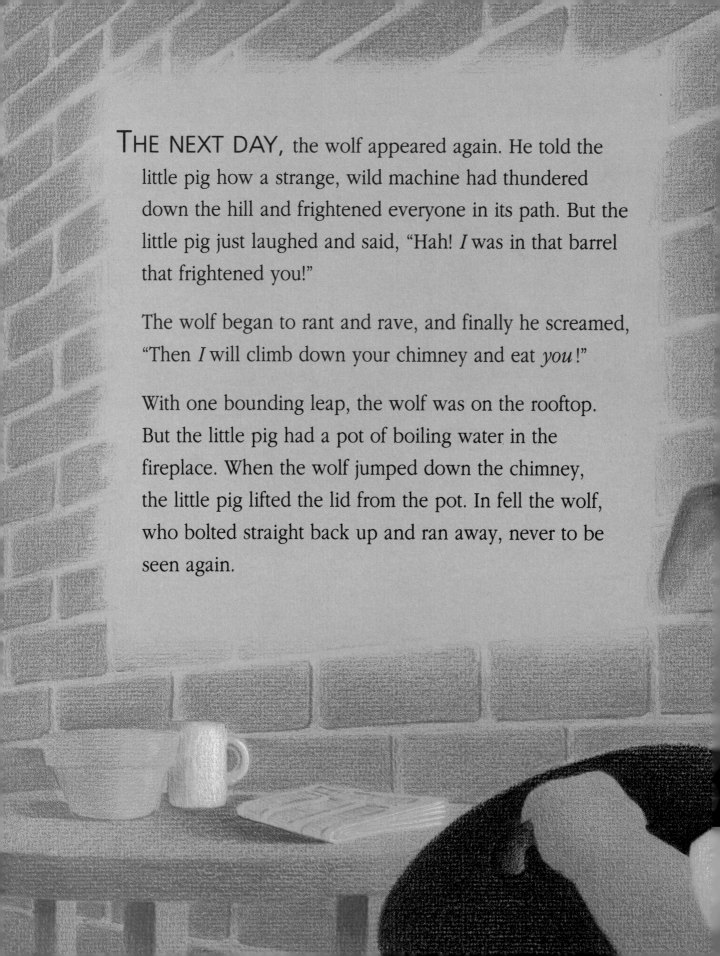

THE NEXT DAY, the wolf appeared again. He told the little pig how a strange, wild machine had thundered down the hill and frightened everyone in its path. But the little pig just laughed and said, "Hah! *I* was in that barrel that frightened you!"

The wolf began to rant and rave, and finally he screamed, "Then *I* will climb down your chimney and eat *you*!"

With one bounding leap, the wolf was on the rooftop. But the little pig had a pot of boiling water in the fireplace. When the wolf jumped down the chimney, the little pig lifted the lid from the pot. In fell the wolf, who bolted straight back up and ran away, never to be seen again.

AND the whole little pig family lived happily ever after in the house made of bricks.

To Parents

Children delight in hearing and reading folk tales. *Three Little Pigs* will
provide your child with an entertaining story as well as a bridge
into learning some important concepts. Here are a few easy and natural
ways your child can express feelings and understandings about the story.
You know your child and can best judge which ideas will
be the most enjoyable.

Act out the scenes with the wolf and the little pigs. For example, start by pretending you're the wolf. Read the wolf's lines and help your child recite the little pigs' answers. Switch roles.

Stuff a sock or other soft object into an empty paper-towel tube. Roll the tube down any slanted surface. Pretend this is the little pig rolling down the hill in a barrel to scare the wolf. Each time you roll the tube, you and your child can make the sounds the little pig and wolf would make.

Wear snout masks when you role-play the three little pigs and the wolf. To make the snouts, cut off the top third of large plastic bleach bottles that have handles. Wash the "snouts" thoroughly. Attach elastic or string to each side. Help your child decorate each snout.

Turn a paper plate or pizza cardboard into a clock to use while sharing the story with your child. Write big numerals on the clock face. With a metal fastener, attach hands cut from stiff paper. Change the time to go with each scene — 6, 5, 4 o'clock and so on. After each change, ask your child to tell what time it is.

Each little pig had help to build a house. Talk with your child about people who help us to do things every day — family, friends, teachers, store clerks, bus drivers, and librarians, for example. Ask what these people do to help us.

Each pig built a different kind of house. Have your child draw a picture of each one of these and of your own house. Make sure to add the street address. Talk with your child about why it's always good to remember your street address.